WALT DISNEY PRODUCTIONS
presents

The Rescuers in
TROUBLE IN DEVIL'S BAYOU

Random House  New York

Devil's Bayou was a swamp.

In the middle of this swamp was a shabby old shack.

Two greedy people, Mr. Snoops and his partner, Madame Medusa, lived in the shack. They did not like living there.

But they knew a pirate's treasure was
buried in the swamp.
Medusa wanted to find it!
Every morning she shouted, "Snoops,
go look for my treasure!"

Then Medusa would climb onto her pet
crocodiles, Brutus and Nero.
She would ride through the swamp
very quickly.

She was so busy looking for the treasure,
that she did not notice what trouble she
caused her neighbors.

She always flooded the swamp folks' houses.

At night Snoops and Medusa kept
their neighbors awake.

Snoops made fireworks so Medusa
had enough light to search for
the treasure.

One night Medusa drove her swamp-mobile
up to an old hollow tree.

She stuck her arm inside the tree trunk.

She felt something....

It was a map—a pirate's map!

An **X** marked the spot where the treasure was hidden.

"I'll be rich!" Medusa cried.

She raced home to show Snoops the map.

They began to search for the treasure
right away.

They walked, and walked, and walked.

At last they reached the spot where the
map said the treasure was buried.

"Hurry up, Snoops!" Medusa shouted.

"Start digging right there!" she said. She did not see the little house of the swamp folks nearby.

Snoops dug for many, many hours.
"Medusa," he said, "I need a rest."
"NO REST!" screamed Medusa.
"We have to find that treasure."

Snoops kept digging.

The pile of dirt got higher,
and higher.

He was covering up the house
of Luke and Ellie May!

"Help!" cried Luke and Ellie May.
Dirt fell from their chimney.
"We'll be buried alive!"

Turtle heard Luke
and Ellie May
call for help.

Mr. Owl ran to tell
Mr. Rabbit.

Mr. Rabbit ran to tell Mr. Evinrude
the dragonfly that Luke and Ellie May
needed help.

Buzz ... buzz!
"I will help Luke and Ellie May," said
Evinrude, "for I am their best friend."
And off he flew!

But Evinrude did not get far.
The bats heard Evinrude's buzz-buzzing.
And bats like dragonflies for dinner!
Squeak...squeak!
The bats ran after Evinrude.

The bats were about to catch him!
But Evinrude reached Luke and
Ellie May's house in time.
He flew straight down their chimney.

"Oh Evinrude!" cried Ellie May. "What can we do?"

"If we don't get rid of that greedy pair, we'll be buried alive in here!" said Luke.

"Don't worry, friends," said Evinrude.

Evinrude packed
his bag and flew out
over the swamp.

"I'll go to the city and find the
Rescuers," he said. "Bernard and
Bianca will know what to do."

Evinrude flew day and night.
He flew through rain and lightning.
When Evinrude reached the city,
it started to snow.

Evinrude found Bernard and Bianca's house.
He knocked at the window.
They were inside drinking hot cocoa.
"Bernard dear," said Bianca, "who is
knocking?"

"It's Evinrude," said Bernard. "He must have flown here from Devil's Bayou!"

Evinrude rested for a minute.

Then he told Bernard and Bianca about the trouble in Devil's Bayou.

"We help anyone, anywhere," said the Rescuers.

They packed their bags quickly.

Then they got the bus to Albatross Airport.

The airport was on a rooftop.

"Trouble in Devil's Bayou?" said
Captain Orville. "Climb aboard."
So Evinrude and the Rescuers
climbed aboard.
Away they flew!

Captain Orville flew over
the city.
Bianca began to smile.
"I LOVE flying!" she said.

Bernard and Evinrude
just held on tight.
They did not like flying
as much as Bianca did!

Soon they came
to the swamp.
Captain Orville
looked for a place
to land.

"Hold onto your hats!" he said.
Then the captain landed with a
great big SPLASH!

The Rescuers went straight to
Luke and Ellie May's house.
Evinrude and Bernard helped
Bianca climb down the chimney.

"We're here to help you!" cried Bianca.
"Don't worry about Snoops and Medusa,"
she said.

"I have a plan to get rid of
them once and for all."

Luke and Bernard dug all the dirt away from the door.

Then Bianca sent Luke and Ellie May to get the things they needed for the plan.

Ellie May got old sheets.

Luke went to find some strong sticks.

All the other swamp folks hurried to Luke's house to help.

"We must be ready tonight," Luke told the swamp folks.

They tied the sticks together.
They put old gloves on the sticks...

Soon they had a real pirate ghost!
Mr. Rabbit crawled under
the sheets and carried
the scary ghost.

Late that night, the ghost found
Mr. Snoops and Madame Medusa.
"Who-o-o, who, who!" wailed the ghost.
"Who is digging for my buried treasure?"
Snoops and Medusa did not wait to answer.

They jumped on Medusa's pet crocodiles
and zoomed away from Devil's Bayou.

All the swamp folks had a good laugh.
They were rid of Snoops and Medusa once
and for all!

Captain Orville
got ready to take off.
Bernard and Bianca
said good-bye to the swamp folks.
"Don't forget," said Bianca and
Bernard, "we help anyone, anywhere."

The trouble in Devil's Bayou was over.

Bernard and Bianca and Captain Orville flew away over the swamp.

They were happy that they had helped their friends.